T0281928

The LIGHTNING CIRCLE

VIKKI VANSICKLE

With Illustrations by
LAURA K. WATSON

tundra

Tundra Books, an imprint of Tundra Book Group,
a division of Penguin Random House of Canada Limited

*Publisher's note: This book is a work of fiction. Names, characters,
places and incidents either are the product of the author's imagination
or are used fictitiously, and any resemblance to actual persons
living or dead, events, or locales is entirely coincidental.*

Library and Archives Canada Cataloguing in Publication

Title: The lightning circle / Vikki VanSickle ; illustrated by Laura K. Watson.
Names: VanSickle, Vikki, 1982- author. | Watson, Laura K., illustrator.
Identifiers: Canadiana (print) 2023019933X | Canadiana (ebook) 20230199348 |
ISBN 9781774882498 (hardcover) | ISBN 9781774882504 (EPUB)
Subjects: LCGFT: Novels in verse.
Classification: LCC PS8643.A59 L54 2024 | DDC jC813/.6—dc23

Published simultaneously in the United States of America by
Tundra Books of Northern New York, an imprint of Tundra Book Group,
a division of Penguin Random House of Canada Limited

Library of Congress Control Number: 2023934497

Edited by Lynne Missen
Designed by Gigi Lau
The artwork in this book was drawn with pencil and colored digitally.
The text was set in Minion Pro.

Printed in China

www.penguinrandomhouse.ca

1 2 3 4 5   28 27 26 25 24

Penguin
Random House
tundra | TUNDRA BOOKS

To the girls and women
of Camp Rim Rock.

2006

Arrival 🍁

I step off the plane
out of the stale air
and breathe in
the very soul
of West Virginia.

A man named Billy
is waiting for me
under a sign that says
Nora Nichols.

He takes my bags
and leads me to a van
with the words
Camp Cradle Rock
printed on the side
in a promising shade of blue.

"You're the only pickup today,"
he says.

In the van, I sit back
and watch the Blue Mountains
rise before me.

I feel like Dorothy
entering the Emerald City.
As we drive through forests
of deepening green,
I hear a hidden river
whispering between the trees.

Suddenly,
the forest clears
and a swath of rippling grass
spreads from the road
to the mountain,
like a tablecloth
set with four riding rings
dotted with horses
too many to count.

From the road
it is difficult to see
the rest of Camp Cradle Rock
nestled in
the dark skirts
of the mountain.

But I feel it there, waiting.

Dropping the Bomb

"Summer camp? Why?"

"It sounded fun."

"But you don't even like camping!"

"It's camp, Kara, not camp-*ing*."

"Nora, have you ever been to camp?
It's all sports and color wars and screaming."

"They have an arts and crafts program.
You know I like to draw."

"I don't get it. This is so not like you."

Kara and I have been
best friends
since the day we wore
the same pink high-tops
to class in third grade.

She knows
almost all there is to know
about me.

But some wounds
are still tender,
and I can't bring myself
to tell her

that I'm suffocating at home,
where I'm reminded of him
at every corner,

where his name
hangs heavy in the air,
like smog.

I need to get away.
Someplace where
the air is clean
and I can breathe deeply
once again.

First Day

Sitting in the dining hall,
at glossy tables painted
happy-face yellow,
staff training begins.

It feels
like the first day of school
and it's hard
to concentrate
on schedules and procedures and rules
surrounded by sixty strangers,
wondering which of them
might become your friends.

Officially,
we'll be divided
by unit and activity.

Unofficially,
we'll divide ourselves
along the invisible, unspoken lines
of coolness.

But for now,
we're one big mass
of possible friendships.

The Ravens' Nest

This summer
I am not a girl
but a raven,
or rather
a keeper of ravens.

At Camp Cradle Rock
the units are named for birds,
from the littlest Chickadees
to the oldest Eagles
and everything in between—
Sparrow, Robin, Warbler, Wren, and

Raven—
the name given
to my assigned unit
and to the thirteen-year-old campers
who will roost here
for the summer.

Twenty-four fledglings
divided among three cabins—
cozy nests
set back in the trees,
each with a porch,
a clothesline,
and a narrow path
that snakes toward
a shared bathroom.

At the very heart of the unit
a group of weathered benches
surrounds a raked firepit.

Kala, our Unit Head,
Queen of Ravens,
strikes a match and
lights the first fire of
the summer.

"Welcome home, Ravens."

Summer Names

None of the counselors
go by their first names.
They unfold their summer names
and step into them
like an old pair of shorts.

Kala
like the ukulele
she slings across her back.

Mezzo
for the parts she sings
in musicals back at home.

Tex
for the state she loves
and the Lone Star tattoo
that ripples across her left biceps.

Gilly
for the gills she should have
given how much time
she spends in the water.

No one explains
why Withers
is Withers,
but I wonder if
it's because her silent stare
can shrivel a person
at a glance.

Kala waves
at the black forest
beyond the firepit.

"Out there you're Nora.
Here you can be
whoever you want.
So, who's it going to be?"

Who I've Been

Nowah.
Because the r in my name
was too hard
for my baby cousin
to pronounce.

No-No.
Because the Robinson kids
didn't like it
when I told them—
No more ice cream before bed.
No, we can't watch Chucky on TV.
No, you can't put the cat in the bath.

Minnie Mouse.
Because of the tiny squeal
I make at the end
of my sneezes.

Nor—
Because he likes to shorten everything
Because friends give each other nicknames
Because when it comes to me,
I'm neither friend
nor girlfriend.

First Night

Eventually
when the campers arrive
we'll be divided in pairs
and assigned a cabin,
but for the first week
Kala has us all sleep
in the same cabin
for bonding reasons.

Conversation
flows light and easy
among the other Ravens
yet I can't find a place
to dip in.

They chat about school
and boyfriends
and bemoan an entire summer
without men.

I thought that was the appeal
of an all-girls camp.

Mezzo, from Georgia,
asks me if there's someone sweet
waiting for me back home.

Something about the warmth
of her sunny drawl
unleashes a flood of homesickness
and all I can do
is shrug.

I'm not sure what I'd say
even if I could speak.

What I Left Behind

Air-conditioning
Sunday matinees with Kara
Strawberry Shine lip gloss
television
minimum wage (plus tips)
Meowzer the cat
the privacy of my own room
email
Sidewalk Sale Days
Mocha Frappuccinos
road trips to the beach
my favorite summer dress
        (the "dry clean only" one)
my name?
boys.

Especially all things
having to do
with one boy
in particular.

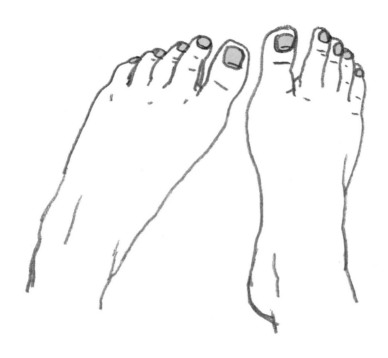

What I've Gained

One green river
two swimming pools
a three-inch-thick manual
starry nights
    (way better than Van Gogh's)
nine roommates
a two-month supply of embroidery floss
a full-serve dining hall
    (with excellent mac and cheese)
access to sixty horses
    (and a fully equipped barn)
a fresh start.

Kala

At six-one
she'll be a foot taller
than the campers
(and most of the staff).

She wears a jade turtle
on a string around her neck,
because
"A turtle carries its home on its
back."

At the end of the summer Kala
is moving to Oregon with her
boyfriend.

She wants to live
among all that green
and make a difference
in the world.

She says it
just like that—
as if making a difference in the world
was something as ordinary
as waitressing
or accounting.

But as impossible as it sounds,
I believe she'll do it.
Kala
is that kind of person.

KALA

Training

All week
we take turns
reading aloud from the manual,
role-playing conflict resolution,
and tending to imaginary ankle sprains.

Some counselors
have been coming here
for years.
They know all the words
to all the songs,
and the exact ratio
of chocolate to marshmallow
in the perfect banana boat.

But to those of us
who are new
the learning curve
feels
steep.

We mumble at singalong,
take a wrong turn on the way to lunch,
and are slow to offer tips
for dealing with homesickness.

"Don't worry,"
everyone says.
"You'll learn."

Meet the Ravens!

Kala tells us
to think of each other
as family,
and the Ravens' Nest
as home.

I awake every morning
to Mezzo singing in the shower.
She likes to keep her voice
in performance shape
and writes out inspirational lyrics
to pin up on the cabin walls.

Withers
came all the way from England
to teach horseback riding.
She keeps to herself.
But when she looks at you
it's like she can see your thoughts
as clearly as freckles.

MEZZO

GILLY

Gilly
is what Kala calls
a "lifer"—
a camper for seven years,
counselor for two,
she lives for the summer
and Camp Cradle Rock.

Mostly I stick with Tex and Mezzo.

When Tex isn't gushing
about her boyfriend Jason
she's pretty fun to be around.
And Mezzo puts me at ease,
like a cup of tea on a rainy day.

WITHERS

At seventeen,
I am the youngest,
the kid sister
in this summer family.

People say you pick your friends
but you can't pick your family.
I wonder if this applies
to camp.

TEX

Initiation

"You're seventeen and you've never been to camp?
Well dang, Nora!
What the heck did you do all summer?"

I point out to Tex
that she's just as new as I am.

"Nuh-uh. I may be new here,
but I've been to lots of other camps.
You're a camp virgin."

Gilly the Lifer
is grinning—
about as friendly
as the Cheshire Cat.
"What should we do to the virgin?"

Tex grabs my hand.
"Whatever you do to her,
you have to do to me, too."

"They used to make new counselors
spend the night
in the graveyard."

"What graveyard?"

Gilly's cat eyes glow.
"You haven't seen it?
If you look closely
you can see three unmarked gravestones
in the woods behind Arts and Crafts."

"You won't see that in the brochure!"

"Or the manual."

"So how about it, ladies?
 Care to spend the night with some ghosts?"

"D'you reckon they're male?"

Just as Tex
turns lily-white
Kala swoops in for the rescue.

"No one is sleeping in the graveyard.
Initiation is for frat boys
and other Neanderthals."

Though I am grateful,
I can't help feeling
like the kid
who has to be bailed out
in the schoolyard
by her older sister.

Gilly pouts.
"Aw, come on, Kala.
Not even a midnight skinny-dip?"

Kala shakes her head.
"I can't have any of you
come down with hypothermia."

Thank god.
I'd take ghosts
over nudity
any day.

Cradle Rock

On the way to breakfast
I ask Kala
where Camp Cradle Rock
gets its name.

She points at the mountain.
"See there?
Between those trees?
That's the cradle."

"I don't see it."

"I didn't either, at first.
But if you look long enough
you'll see the shape of a cradle
in those rocks right there."

"I still don't see it."

"Keep looking."

There is something nice
about the name
Cradle Rock
even if I can't yet
see it myself.

Like the earth
is ready to catch us
in her solid arms of stone,
while the wind
whispers mountain lullabies
in our ears.

Willpower

I will not think
about him today.

I will not imagine my return,
strong and lean
from three months
traipsing up and down a mountain,
confidence glowing like a tan,
dazzling him
with the new me.

I will not think about it
for
one
single
second.

This summer
is not about
him,

it's about
me.

Shells

I am collecting shells
from the riverbank.

I nudge them loose
with my toe
and rinse the sand away
in the warm, shallow water.

On the outside
they are rough to touch.
Rings of browns
in caramels and chocolates
flaking off.
Nothing much to look at.

But the insides,

the insides are silky
violet with swirls
of pearl and lavender.

Never Have I Ever

Huddled around
the dying fire,
the game begins.

We all start
with ten fingers
spread before us.

Then someone
makes a confession.
If you've done it
you pull in a finger.

Never have I ever—
stolen a lip gloss
smoked weed
had outdoor sex.

A full hand
represents
all the things
you have not done.

As the fingers disappear
and the confessions get wilder,
I feel more and more
like a child
than a so-called peer
of these counselors.

At the end of the game
I stare at my ten fingers
and wonder—
what wisdom can I possibly offer
the girls in my cabin?

And I am thankful
for the heat of the fire,
which flushes all our cheeks.

Peeing at Midnight

At night,
the naked yellow bulbs
in the bathroom
glow like owl eyes
in the darkness.

Something crashes through the trees
—a clumsy squirrel
or panicked deer—
and I hurry along the path

telling myself those black things
are sticks,
not snakes,

and vow never to take
even a single sip of water
past eight o'clock
for the rest of the summer.

Breast Friends

"You have perfect bikini boobs."
Tex is staring
at my chest.

Withers and Mezzo
look up from Poolside Safety
to see for themselves.

I blush
and resist the urge
to cover my breasts
with my hands.

Withers nods.
"They're a good set of tits."

Tex shudders.
"Ugh. I hate the word tit."

Mezzo agrees.
"Tits, boobs, toddies, whatever you call them,
Nora's got herself a nice pair."

Nice?
Nice boobs
fit perfectly
into measured cup sizes
and behave themselves
in strapless dresses.

My breasts are at best
enthusiastic.
At worst,
downright unruly.

Tex cups her own breasts and sighs.
"I'd give anything
for your lovely ladies."

"Me too," says Mezzo.
"So you better show them off.
If not for you, then for us."

Tex agrees.
"You owe it
to small-breasted women everywhere."

Mezzo raises a bottle
of sunscreen
in a toast.
"Here's to Nora,
champion and advocate
for big tits."

"Mezzo!"

"Fine. Bounteous breasts."

"Better."

Gilly calls over
from the lifeguard tower.
"I hope y'all are studying
your aquatics manuals!"

"Don't worry,"
says Tex.
"We were just going over
the breaststroke."

Food

You'd think
we were a bunch
of pregnant women
the way we talk about food.

I defend the right
to accent my mac and cheese
with ketchup

and try not to stare
as Mezzo loads her sandwich
with potato chips.

Gilly is not so subtle.
"Chips aren't a filling, Mezzo.
They're a side dish."

"You ever tried it?"

"Never have, never will."

Withers came from England prepared,
stocked with Cadbury Buttons
and Marmite
and PG Tips tea
which she trades
by the bag.

Just about the only thing we agree on
is that Cadbury's English chocolate
far outranks anything Hershey
has ever come up with.

Withers slathers her toast
with Marmite,
black as tar,
and offers me the first bite.

"Here. A little taste of heaven,
direct from the British Isles."

Kala intervenes.

"You might try it
with a bit of honey.
Soften the blow."

I try not to gag
and offer the toast
to Mezzo.

"Nuh-uh. I'd rather starve.
You try, Tex!"

Tex considers
the sad little piece of toast
that looks like it's been salvaged
from an oil spill.

"I think I've lost my appetite."

Gilly rolls her eyes. "What appetite?"

Tex frowns.
"I'm not a big eater."

All she's had to eat is
a spoonful of tuna
and three sticks of celery.

Gilly continues.
"Wait till camp starts.
You'll be so hungry
you'll eat anything."

"Even Marmite?"

"I promise you, Withers,
I will never
in a million years
be that hungry."

The Collector

I collect words
like some people collect
beach glass,

swirling them round and round
till they feel smooth
against my cheek.

I kept his words
on the tip of my tongue
and whispered them
over and over
until they lulled me to sleep
like waves on the sand.

But now,
those same words
keep me up at night

wondering how
they could have been used
so carelessly.

Kara says
I give other people's words
too much weight.

Maybe the problem is
that some people
don't give them enough.

Radiant

Side by side
at a table outside the gym
taking tickets
for the semiformal.

"Thanks, bro! Nora here
will give you a coat check ticket.
Doesn't she look radiant tonight?"

Radiant.
A word reserved
for the sun
and angels
and other things
that give off light.

But never
for an ordinary,
unremarkable,
earthly girl
like me.

Radiant.

I took it in
and savored it,
letting its surprising flavor
burst on my tongue.

The syllables dissolved
and whizzed through my bloodstream
like champagne bubbles.

Rising to the surface,
they cobbled my skin
and speckled my eyes
with light.

And I felt
radiant.

Folk Songs

At night,
bent over her ukulele,
Kala teaches us
the kind of songs
you'd find on an old record album
or a crackly AM station
in the middle of the night.

Deep in the woods,
the lyrics pulse with new life
and I get their folksy wisdom
for the first time.

Only love can break your heart.
The first cut is the deepest.
I really don't know love at all.

I stare into the fire
for so long
that the heat scours my brain,
and when I finally lie back
in the cool grass
the only ghosts
are the burning ghosts of flames
that dance between the stars.

A Little White Lie

"Truth, dare, double-dare, promise to repeat."

"We aren't seriously playing this, are we?"

"It's tradition, Withers!"

"Nothing too crazy, Gilly."

"Don't worry, Kala."

"Fine. Truth."

The Cheshire Cat is at it again.

"Tex. How many guys have you slept with?"

"Gilly!"

"She said truth!"

"No, no, it's fine. Just the one, just Jason."

Mezzo grins. "Mine's four."

"Why am I not surprised?"

A pillow sails
across the room
on a stiff breeze of laughter
and lands at Mezzo's feet.

"Nora.
Truth, dare,
double-dare,
promise to repeat."

"Truth."

"More truth? You guys are no fun."

"I'll remember that
when it's your turn, Gilly!
Nora, have you ever been in love?"

Have I ever been in love?
Yes.

"Well?"

Yes.

"Have you?"

"No."

"You will be. Hang in there!"

"You're better off, mate.
Who needs a man!"

"I do."

"Me too!"

"I miss Jason."

"Enough with the Jason talk, Tex."

I bow out of the game
and hide behind my book
unnoticed

save for Withers,
who won't
stop
staring.

Qualified

In a few short days
my cabin will be full
of thirteen-year-old girls,
looking to me for support
and entertainment
and leadership.

I have to wonder
if I'm qualified for all that.
I know the actions
to fifteen camp songs,
how to light a fire,
and administer CPR.

But how do I teach them
to go out into the world,
to take risks,
to fall in love?

I went out on that limb
everyone is always talking about,
and I'm still recovering
from the fall.

What Tex Wants

"When I go home,
I'm going to be
thin, blond, and brown."

Tex is sprawled on her towel,
baby-oiled skin
glistening in the sun,

a half-empty
bottle of Sun-In
at her side.

"The sun is strongest
between eleven and two,"
she says.

I already know this.
That's why we have
indoor activities then.

She triple-rolls her waistband
and wears strapless bikini tops
to get maximum "brownage."

"What about cancer?"

"We're all going to die someday, Nora.
And I'd rather die
thin, blond, and brown."

Living Assignments

Today Kala tells us
who will live
in which cabin
for the rest of the summer.

I make a silent wish
for Tex or Mezzo.
I don't dare hope for Kala.
Gilly is a bit too cold
and Withers
makes me nervous.

"Here we go, Ravens.
Cabin One, myself and Gilly.
Cabin Two, Mezzo and Tex.
Cabin Three, Nora and Withers.
That reminds me, Nora.
You need to pick a camp name!"

Everyone seems pleased.
There's lots of hugging
and squealing.

My stomach burns
as Tex and Mezzo rush off
to make plans.

We used to make plans
together.

Withers is looking at me.
"Well then.
Come on, Miss Nora.
Let's get settled."

I smile,
hoping it's bright enough
to blind her X-ray vision
from seeing
my disappointment.

Withers

Withers
is a self-proclaimed
"horsey person."

It turns out her name
is not a reference
to her powerful stare
but to the ridge between
the shoulder blades
of a horse.

"What else would it mean?"
she snorts.

If she doesn't know
I'm not going to tell her.

She gets up before dawn
to bring the horses in,
and stays late
to wash them down,
muck out the stalls,
and do other barn stuff.

She doesn't talk much
and hates the singing
and the shouting
parts of camp.
But at twenty-six
she's the oldest counselor
and the one who's been here
the longest.

I ask her why she comes back
year after year.

"Because camp is cleansing."

"Cleansing?"

"Yes, cleansing."

Withers looks into my face
and something she sees
makes her smile.

She brushes my arm
in a gesture that might be
affectionate.

"You'll see."

An Afternoon in Arts and Crafts

I'm alone
for the first time
in days,
sorting through shelves,
counting art supplies,
ticking off boxes.

Tempera paints?
Check.
Two rolls of brown kraft paper?
Check check.

I was looking forward
to the alone time,
but without the others
to distract me,
thoughts of him
come roaring in
and I'm washed out to sea
on a relentless tide
of longing.

Stranded,
I pray for the dinner bell
to bring me back
to the others
and my senses.

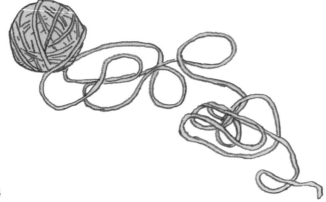

Maybe

All day long
 the others ask,
"Have you picked a camp name yet?"

But what they're asking is,
 "Do you know who you are yet?"

As if the answer to that
is simple.

I know what I want to be—
someone braver,
someone funnier,
someone beloved.

Maybe Sharpie—
playful, bright,
a permanent mark
on your life.

Maybe Sketch,
for the drawings I make
in my journal.

Maybe Shell,
unremarkable on the outside,
whirling, swirling, hopeful
underneath.

Maybe Canuck,
a nod to where I'm from—
who doesn't love
a Canadian?

At night
even the owls call—
who, who, who!
I want to shout back,
you tell me!

Nesting

After two weeks
I'm still not used
to sleeping on that plastic pancake
they call a mattress.

"Oi, Nora. You look horrible.
Not sleeping well?"

Withers sleeps like the dead.
Except I'm not sure the dead
would make as much noise.

"No, not really."

"You need an egg crate."

"A what?"

Later,
I return to the cabin to find
a thick slab of dimpled foam
lying on my bed,
next to an extra pillow.

"That, Miss Nora,
is an egg crate."

"Where did you get it?"

"When you've worked here
as long as I have,
you learn a few things."

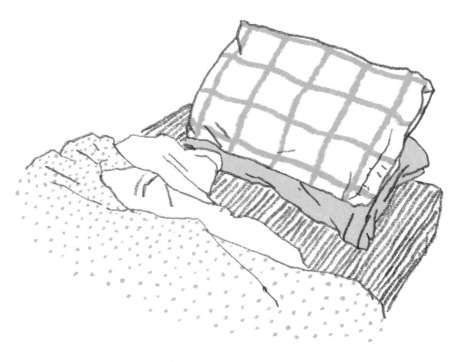

Withers shows me
how to secure the egg crate
to the mattress,
dimpled side up.

That night
in my new cushy bed
I sleep like the dead.

Withers says
I snore loud enough
to wake them.

Withers on Riding

Withers cannot believe
I've never been on a horse.
But the way she talks about riding,
I might be convinced.

"A horse doesn't care
what you look like,
who you are,
or whether you're a boy or girl.

Riding can be especially powerful
for a girl who feels
like she has no control
in her life,

because if she can learn to control
such a powerful animal,
then maybe
she can learn to control
other things, too."

Withers looks at me
and smiles.

"So, Miss Nora.
When are we going
to get you on a horse?"

The Lightning Circle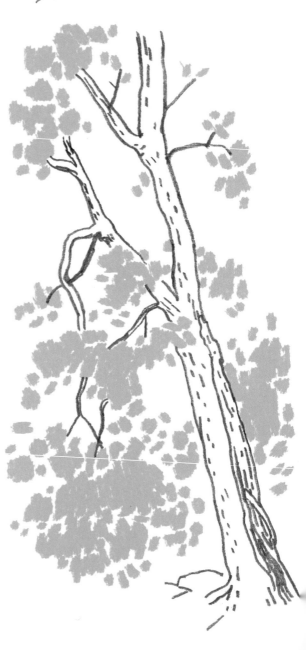

After an hour
of uphill scrambling
over the scarred face
of the rim rocks,
Kala leads us
to a ledge
free of pine needles
and exposed, ropy roots.

The remains of a tree,
split down the middle,
jut forth from the rock.

"Fifty years ago
a group came up
here on a hike,
when a storm came
over the mountain
without warning.

The rain made
it too slick
to hike back down,
so they stayed here,
joined hands,
and sang songs
to keep the campers
from being frightened.

Lightning struck
this tree
right here.

It traveled down
through the trunk
and into the roots that
one camper was
standing on.

The charge that
entered her body
passed through
the entire circle.

She broke the circle
and fell to the ground,
unconscious.

The counselors
administered CPR
for one hour
until the ambulance arrived.

When she woke up
there was no lasting damage,
except a streak of white
in her hair.

The rescue workers said
if the girls hadn't
been holding hands
the shock would have been
too much
for one body.

She would
have died
instantly."

At this point
Kala leads us
in forming
a lightning circle
of our own.
Six women,
twelve hands,
and the feeling that passes
from hand to hand
is something like
electricity.

Nova

Picking our way
back down the rim rocks,
still buzzing,
I announce,
"I decided on my camp name."

Tex claps.
Kala smiles.
Mezzo says,
"Drumroll, please."

"From now on,
You can call me
Nova."

Nova.
Like Nora, but not.
Trading in the
hooked r—
that rusty, guttural, swashbuckling letter—
for a quietly dignified v.

I watch my new name
settle over everyone
like an idea.

"Awesome!"

"Nova is cool as hell."

"Nova as in new, the new Nora, I like it."

Gilly frowns.

"It's not that different.
It's basically your name,
but with a v."

I'm not sure how to say
that I like the softness
of the v on my lips
and how the word
—Nova—
feels like a wish.

So I shrug.
"I just like the way it sounds."

All the way back
the others shout out
as many v words
as they can name.

V for victory!
V for voluptuous!
Vanilla! Vodka! Visionary! Virgin!

It's a game,
like everything else here,
but one I feel a part of.

Already, I feel different.
Nora observed.
Nova belongs.

JuLy
2006

Opening Day

We wait
on the benches
around the firepit
for the campers to arrive.

Already it's hot.

My staff shirt feels stiff,
and the Opening Day brunch
isn't sitting well
in my stomach.

To distract myself,
I fashion an elaborate chore wheel
using glitter pens
and a hole punch
(the one shaped like a unicorn).

Kala returns
from her Unit Head meeting
looking like a counselor from a magazine,
complete with a whistle
and clipboard.

She hands out the bedcharts
and I pore over the list
searching for clues
to what the summer holds.

All the list tells me
are the names and ages
of the girls in my cabin.

I say them in my head
over and over
until they are etched in my memory
like the black lines of a coloring book
waiting to be filled in.

Donyelle

"Welcome to Cradle Rock.
I'm Nova. And you are?"

"Donyelle.
You can cut the happy camper shit.
I didn't even want to come this year.
Do you have a boyfriend?"

My smile freezes
as all the greetings
we rehearsed at pre-camp
crack and shatter
against her hard exterior.

Donyelle,
with her purple eyeliner
and breezy skirt,
throws her bag on a bunk
then stares me down.
"Well? Do you?"

"No."

Donyelle sighs
and flips through
a magazine.

"I've been having sex for months now.
So this summer is going to be, like,
really hard for me."

Though she is younger
I falter in the presence of a
girl so effortlessly cool.

I don't know what I expected
from my first encounter with a camper.

But I didn't expect it
to be about boys.

Kim and Becca

I'm Kim.

I'm Becca.

We met at camp

but we're from the same city.

Weird, hey?

Weird!

We request each other—

every year.

We're always in

the same cabin. I'm top bunk

and I'm bottom.

This is our sixth

No, seventh—

No, sixth—

But what about the year—

That doesn't count,
it was just one week.

Okay, sixth.

Sixth summer. We mark the days—

on a calendar

before camp.

Starting after
Spring Break

till now!

Like those
Christmas calendars.

Advent calendars!

Yeah, advent calendars

but without chocolates.

We should get chocolates!

Totally!

Totally.

Is Palais here?

Yeah, Palais!

She was the best—

The best

No pressure.

We don't do pranks
on counselors
or anything.

No, not anymore.

So over.

the best summer yet!

the best counselor we ever had.

Yeah, no pressure.

Well, not anymore.

We're so over that!

This is going to be the best—

Totally!

Abby

"Cool chore wheel!
Did you make it?"

"I did."

Camper number four
is all braces
and dimples
and apple cheeks.

Her trunk is red
and covered in
stickers and signatures
from past summers.

She is the first to notice
my daily schedule,
lavishly lettered
and posted for all to see.

"Can you teach me to write
all cool and swirly like that?"

"Sure. It looks harder than it is."

"Awesome.
I'm Abby."

"I'm Nova."

We make her bed
and I start to feel
like a real counselor.
All cool and swirly.

The Incredible Rubber Counselor

Casey, Rachel, and Alex
arrive at the same time.

With Withers on barn duty,
it's just me here
to welcome everyone.
I bounce back and forth
like a rubber ball
helping them get settled
and reminding them of
swim evaluations
in twenty minutes.

Above her bunk
Casey papers the ceiling
with creased centerfolds
from teen magazines.

Within seconds
Rachel scurries over
to confess her undying love
for some Disney Channel heartthrob
in one of Casey's posters.

Alex lines up her shoes
in a neat row beside her trunk
and tucks her sheets in tightly,
military style.

They settle in,
and still I bounce between them
feeling anything
but settled.

Another Beginning

Just when I got a handle
on all the staff,
my head swims
with the names and faces
of my new campers.

They look younger
than I expected,
though they are trying hard
to look older.

All of a sudden
camp is alive
in a way that it
never was before,

buzzing with new energy
that reverberates like music
in the stones of Cradle Rock.

ABBY

DONYELLE

Pool Politics

At swim evaluations,
Donyelle refuses
to get into the pool.

"I have my period," she says,
barely glancing up
from a magazine.

It crosses my mind
that a girl who has been
having sex for a year
can surely manage a tampon.

But I don't say this.
Because I don't know her
    (and it might not be true).
Because I am a counselor
    (and I will not be provoked).
Because Nora dwells,
but Nova rises above.

Instead,
I smile brightly,
with all my teeth.

"No problem. Next time, maybe."

Donyelle snorts.

"Doubtful."

Highs / Lows

"Are we going to do highs/lows?"

"I love highs/lows."

"Palais always did them—"

"every night before lights-out."

"Can we please?"

"Pleeeeeease?"

How can I refuse?

"Wicked!"

"Wicked!"

"I'll start. My high was the first campfire of the summer—"

"Mine too!"

"And my low was finding out that Palais didn't come back."

"Bummer."

"Major bummer."

The girls go round the room
sharing their high points
and low points.

Heather
(the latecomer)
pretends to be asleep
and Donyelle
refuses to participate.

When it's my turn,
I tell them the whole day
was one long high point.

I don't mention
my growing dislike of this Palais
I keep hearing so much about,
or my failure to win over Donyelle,
or that coming here
may have been a huge mistake.

One day down, forty-one to go.

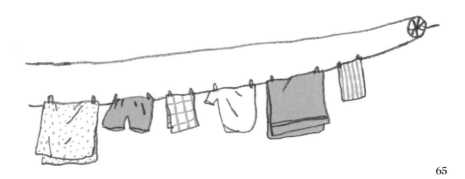

Becca's Guide to Friendship Bracelets

"First, pick your colors.
That might sound easy,
but you're going to have to
look at those colors
for the rest of the summer.
So pick wisely.

Once you've done that,
make a loop
and tape it to something,
like your trunk or your bed.

It's really important
to leave enough string
to tie a good knot,
because with all the swimming
and showering and stuff
the bracelet is going to stretch out.

Most importantly,
you cannot ever take a friendship bracelet off
until the end of camp.

It doesn't matter
how disgusting it gets.
Those are the rules."

Candy Bandits

"Candy may not be stored inside the sleeping cabins."
(Camp Cradle Rock Staff Manual, page 16)

Every bar or bag
of sweet contraband
must be labeled
and locked away safely
in a Rubbermaid container
called the candy bin.

Lid locked carefully in place,
wrapped in a bungee cord,
then topped with a brick—

yet it takes the raccoons
only one night of reconnaissance
to break in.

On the second night,
there is a crash
and the sound
of scampering feet.

We rush out to find
the candy bin on its side,
a rainbow of sweets
spilling onto the grass.

Above us, in the trees,
the raccoons twitter,
gorging themselves on candy
and tossing empty Starburst wrappers
at our heads.

Heather

Heather wears undershirts
instead of underwire
and believes in happy endings.

She hangs a Mickey Mouse towel
from the bunk above her bed
like a curtain.

During activities
she smiles,
sometimes even laughs.

But at every unorganized moment
she retreats behind her curtain
while the other girls chat,
trading candy and secrets.

Ten minutes before lights-out
I pull Mickey aside
and find Heather,
eyes red and streaming.

"I miss my dad."

A letter
written in a shaky hand
lies on the pillow.

Along the bottom
Xs and Os
are strung like beads
in a necklace of longing.

"The other girls don't like me."

This isn't exactly true.
It's not that they don't like Heather.
They just forget about her,
hiding behind Mickey Mouse.

"I don't think I can stay here all summer."

I rub her back
and tell her the first week
is always the hardest.

We make a deal.
She promises
to try to enjoy herself,
and I promise
to check in with her every night.

"Feeling better?"

She nods.
The strange thing is,
so am I.

HEATHER

A Dose of Sunshine

Abby bounces through the day
like a big happy puppy,
full of boundless joy.

Absolutely everyone
is drawn to her,
infected
by her sunny good humor.

But for some reason,
she is drawn
to me.

She skips along beside me
and sits with me at meals
talking in exclamation marks
about her sisters! her horse! her friends!

I teach her calligraphy
and how to fold frogs
out of shining Japanese paper.

She folds and creases
with such enthusiasm,
it almost breaks my heart.

With Abby around
it's hard to feel anything
but sunny.

Arts and Crafts

For half a day
I follow the girls
from activity to activity,
a cheerleader,
a lookout,
a mediator.

But the afternoons
are spent in my second home,
the Arts and Crafts Pavilion,
built into the mountain
at the highest point of camp.

Where the rafters are strung
with a rainbow of tie-dyed T-shirts
drip-drying in the
minted sunlight.

Where the shelves overflow
with mottled gray creatures
emerging from lumps of clay.

Where glitter is locked
away from the sparkle fiends
who would bedazzle the earth
if they could.

Where for a few hours each day
I speak to the girls
in the language
of color, shape, and texture.

And they listen.

Rachel vs. The Mosquitoes

For someone who has spent
five summers at camp,
Rachel sure hates bugs.

At night,
she sets her lantern
in the middle of the room
wrapped in double-sided tape.

"It's a death trap," she explains.
"A bug catching and killing machine.
They head toward the light
then get stuck in the tape and die."

I tell her that sounds
pretty barbaric.

"More barbaric than sucking blood?"

She has a point.
At last count,
I had fifteen
mosquito bites.

"Plus it doubles as a night-light!"

Donyelle rolls over
and gives her unofficial blessing.
"You have to admit, it's pretty genius."

Rachel beams
bright as the death-trap/night-light
and skips back to her bunk
to dream sweet dreams
of a bug-free cabin.

Three Heads Are Scarier than One

Donyelle wields
her nail polish brush
like a scepter,
knighting the chosen ones
in various shades of pink.

On her own
Donyelle is bad enough.
But with Casey and Rachel
she is invincible.

They link arms
and strut through camp,
a three-headed monster
with matching nails
daring anyone
to get in the way.

Dining Hall Madness

When the dining bell tolls
they emerge from all over—
the woods, the pool, the riding ring—
and pour into the dining hall
to shout their way through grace
and collapse into a seat.

They eat with their fingers
and talk with their mouths full,
challenging each other
to chicken nugget eating contests.

Between bites
they slap the table
and clap their hands
to the latest mealtime beat.

We are table number four,
number four, number four!
We are table number four,
calling number ten!

At the end of the meal,
they wriggle through announcements
like schoolkids on Fridays
eager to be set free
to enjoy the rest of the day.

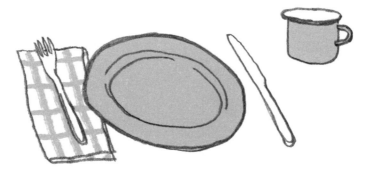

Siesta

After lunch
we laze about the cabin,
the woods steaming
around us.

Bellies full
of grilled cheese sandwiches
and carrot sticks,

yet I hear the whisper
of candy wrappers
from somewhere
across the room.

Crinkle, giggle, crunch.

The girls shimmy up
the bedposts
and drape themselves
across the top bunks
and each other.

They laugh and chatter
like monkeys,
sketching Sharpie tattoos,
munching chocolate contraband.

Crinkle, giggle, crunch.

The air is thick
with the heady scent
of sunscreen
and sweaty
sleeping bags.

This,
plus the heat,
clouds my head
and I succumb
to the delicious embrace
of summer drowsiness.

CASEY

ALEX

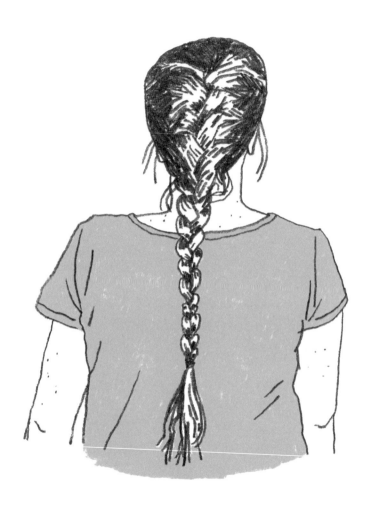

Hair

At first
they tried taming their hair
with the usual assortment
of gels and creams and sprays.

But the swimming
and the sweating
and the humidity
gets the best of them
and their hair follicles.

Suddenly,
French braids
are cool again.

They keep the hair
out of their faces
and off their necks.

But no matter how tightly
the braid is woven,
by the end of the day
wisps escape
and curl round their heads
in fuzzy halos.

Ring Lesson

Withers stands
in the middle of the ring
and conducts a lesson
on sitting trot.

I rarely see her
now that camp is in session
and she spends most of her time
here or in the barn.

After weeks of
direct sunlight
she is brown and gleaming,
like the bays in her ring.

The horses kick up dust
as they trot by me,
a lookout,
leaning against the fence.

I have to squint in the sunlight
to see the girls bobbing atop their steeds
like ducklings tossed between
powerful rippling flanks.

They frown in concentration
and don't acknowledge
my gestures
of encouragement—
a wave, a smile, a thumbs-up.

In the ring, the world simplifies
to girl, horse, sun, dust,
and not much else.

After seventy sweaty minutes
the girls dismount
and lead their horses
back to the barn.

I trail along behind them,
not wanting to disrupt
the connection that flows
between each girl
and her horse

shimmering
like heat waves
in the three o'clock sun.

Unmerciful Sleep

During the day,
I do my best
to control my thoughts.

But at night
my good sense shuts down
and I'm at the mercy
of my stupid, swollen heart,
seeping all over my dreams
and staining my sleep.

He walks into my dreams, uninvited,
strolling right through the mind blocks
I've spent all day building,

and in the morning
I have to start again
from square one.

Bathroom Duty

On Tuesdays, Thursdays, and Saturdays
I clean the bathrooms
with Tex and Mezzo.

Mezzo and I do the toilets
and sweep the bugs off the floor
while Tex cleans the showers
and polishes the sinks.

Mezzo finds black rubber gloves,
with rhinestone-studded cuffs.
"If we have to clean toilets,
at least we can do it in style."

Tex sets up her stereo,
and suddenly bathroom duty
feels more like a dance party.

We shout to each other
above the noise
of the music
and the scrubbing
and the running water

until the other campers wander in,
curious to see
what could possibly be
so much fun
about cleaning the bathrooms.

Afterwards,
we rinse away all that bleach
with the hose
and survey our work.

"Go team go!"
 says Tex.
"Next time,
 I'll bring face masks."

A Fit of Giggles

At least once a day
I am overcome
with a fit of giggles.

You never know
where it will come from—
a well-timed joke,
a pitch-perfect impression,
a silly facial expression.

But every time
I laugh so hard
I have to sit down
and just let it out.

By the end of it
my eyes are streaming,
my cheeks hurt,
and my stomach aches.

Who needs sit-ups
when you've got the giggles?

Alex and Gilly

Alex follows Gilly
like a shadow.
They talk about swim times
and basketball
and the lack of protein
in camp food.

Lately, Alex has taken
to spending siesta
in Cabin One
with Gilly.

The first few times
Abby asked
where Alex had gone.

Now she doesn't bother.

When it's time for activities,
I go to retrieve Alex
and pretend not to hear
when she tells Gilly,
"I wish I was in your cabin."

I tried to talk to Alex
about batting averages
and Mia Hamm,
but we both know
I can't tell the Mets
from the Leafs.

Gilly says,
"Maybe you should get to know
 the girls in your cabin."

Before Alex can protest, Gilly continues.

"And give Nova another try.
 She may not be a sports nut,
 but that doesn't mean
 she isn't a cool person."

Alex agrees to try,
 but only because Gilly
 asked her to.

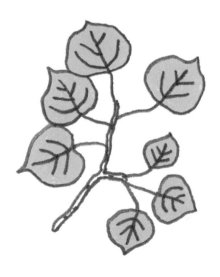

Twins

On the way back
from Performing Arts,
Abby asks
if I will be her twin
at the Twin Dinner.

"We both have brown hair
that curls in the same way,
and we can wear the tie-dyed shirts
we made in Arts and Crafts last week."

I tell her it's the best idea
I've heard all day.

Pool Politics II

"I'm not going in."
Donyelle lounges
at the side of the pool,
a single toe rippling the water.

That is as much of her
that's entered the pool
for the past two weeks.

She glances at Rachel and Casey,
who chime in.
"Me neither."

"We have our periods. You can't make us."

Gilly raises an eyebrow.
"All of you?"

Donyelle flashes a million-dollar smile.
"We're all synced up."

Gilly bristles,
her lifeguard's whistle
clenched between her teeth.
"You can't have your period all summer."

Donyelle shrugs
and resumes tanning.

Rachel and Casey look on
as the other girls splash around,
escaping the heat
and the strict code of conduct that comes
with being Donyelle's chosen ones.

Ties of Friendship

Before the Twin Dinner,
Abby approaches
with the final touch.

"I made one for each of us."

She opens her fist
revealing two bracelets
curled like caterpillars
in her hand.

They look exotic,
in bold stripes of
black, yellow, and lime green.

I tie one around her wrist
and she knots the other
around mine

where it will stay
for the rest of the summer.

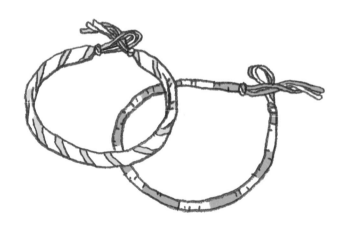

Doughboy Denial

As the girls run off
their sugar high
in the dusky fields
before lights-out,
the counselors help themselves
to the campfire leftovers.

"Not even one little bite?"

Gilly offers Tex
a golden doughboy
roasted to perfection
and dipped in cinnamon sugar.

But Tex says no.

Tex always
says
no.

"I'm worried about her,"
Mezzo whispers.
"She barely eats enough
to keep a fly alive."

Gilly shrugs
and licks the sugar
from her fingers.
"Not everyone likes batter
dipped in butter
and rolled in sugar."

But we all know
it's more than that.
And the truth
hangs heavy in the air between us
like thunderclouds.

Hunger

Watching the girls at mail time
is like watching lions
gather for a feast.

They fall upon the mailbag,
ripping it to pieces
like a carcass,

and slink off to savor
every bite
from home.

Kara's letters from home
are bloodless.
No mention of him,
just like I told her.

But
(secretly)
I'd hoped for something—
a little taste
to kill the craving.

Instead,
I put each of Kara's letters aside,
still hungry.

Happy Endings

I saw Heather
reading every minute
she could.

We traded favorites,
and soon
we couldn't wait
to talk about books
over gooey marshmallows.

We cried through
Walk Two Moons,
and sighed through
The Secret Life of Bees.
Swam through *Olive's Ocean,*
and ran through *Heartbeat.*

When things get rough,
Heather reaches for a book,
taking comfort in a sunny ending
tied up in a big yellow bow.

Rarely in life
do things ever really end.

Let alone
happily.

Nightly Meeting

At half past ten,
campers in bed,
the Raven ladies
gather round
the glowing remains
of the campfire
to talk about the day.

Now that camp is in session
it feels like we never see each other.

It's nice to enjoy
each other's company
in the fading firelight.

One story
sparks another
and conversation flows
like electricity
round our little
lightning circle.

When I return to my cabin
hours later
I don't feel tired
but recharged.

Ready for tomorrow
and whatever
it may bring.

Lionel

Lionel
the rat snake
spends his days
sunning on the grass
or coiled around
the bathroom stairs.

Lionel
is six feet long
and thick
like rubber tubing.

"Rat snakes are harmless,"
Kala reminds us.
"He's more afraid of you
than you are of him."

Withers
is not so patient.

LIONEL

After three days
of campers squealing
to and from the bathroom

she marches out and
yanks Lionel from
his slumber,
pitching him
far into the woods.

The girls watch from
the cabin windows,
cheering her on.

"Withers is my hero,"
says Rachel.

I have to agree.
Watching five-foot Withers
toss a six-foot snake
is more than cool.

Full Moons

"Heads up, Ravens.
The moon is full tonight.
Get ready for the madness."

Tex laughs,
mistaking Mezzo's warning
for a joke.

But Gilly agrees.
"It's true.
Ask any ER nurse—"

"—or school principal—"

"—they'll tell you
people do strange things
on full moons."

"Nonsense,"
says Kala.
"A full moon
is a wishing moon."

I have my own reasons
for avoiding full moons
and keep my eyes down—
preferring to gaze
into the fire.

The Man in the Moon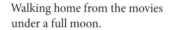

Walking home from the movies
   under a full moon.

"He looks happy tonight."

"Who?"

"The Man in the Moon.
   Look, you can see his face."

I squinted
and tilted my head,
looking for signs of life—
the eyes, the nose, the mouth
he swore looked down at us—
but all I saw
were shadows and smudges,
a Magic Eye puzzle
I couldn't read.

"I'll show you."

He stood behind me
and pointed my arm skyward.
Together we traced
the eyes, the nose, the mouth
and suddenly I saw him—
The Man in the Moon—
silent witness
to the most magical moment
of my life.

I pretended not to see
the eyes, the nose, the mouth
of the man etched in the moon,
so I could feel
the breath, the hand, the heat
of the man behind me
for just a moment longer.

How can I ever
look at the full moon
without seeing a face,
or thinking of the man
who taught me to see it?

An Act of War

Sometime between
sports and riding
Cabin Two decided
they had it out for us.

We returned to find
water bottles, bugspray, and sneakers
duct-taped to the ceiling,
and the number 2
in shaving cream
melting on the floor.

Casey scrambles into the rafters
to peel her belongings
off the ceiling,
rallying the troops.

"This means war!"

"We could wrap their stuff in plastic wrap."

"Or sneak in during breakfast
to mess up their cabin before inspection."

"What if we took their laundry
off the line and threw it in the river?"

"Or the water trough in the barn!"

General Casey lands with a grunt
and rolls the duct tape into
a sticky silver cannonball.

"We need a plan,"
she says.

Page twenty-six
of the Camp Cradle Rock Staff Manual
strongly advises
against pranks
of any kind,
but it fails to mention
that nothing brings people together
like a common purpose.

And as the girls work together
and "Operation Smackdown" unfolds,
complete with diagrams, lookouts, and code words,
I can't help thinking
that Cabin Two started it.

Loyalty

At dinner,
I pass the peas to Mezzo
and wonder if I should warn her
about Operation Smackdown
about to take place in her cabin.

But I worry
about what General Casey
will do to traitors

and remain
silent.

Operation Smackdown

At 8:50 p.m. sharp
Becca comes screaming
from the bathroom.

"Snake! Snake!"

The cabins empty
as everyone rushes out
to hear
how long,
how black,
how scaly.

No one notices
that her hands cover a smirk,
or that Rachel and Casey
have snuck off.

We check the bathroom
and discover that the snake
"at least six feet long"
is gone.

Kala tells everyone
it was probably just Lionel
and that he won't hurt them,
and the girls head back to their cabins.

When I get to mine
it's practically empty
save for Alex, Abby,
and Heather,
giggling madly.

"Everyone's in position,"
says Alex.

"Operation Smackdown is a go."

The Haunting of Cabin Two

In the darkness,
a door slams.

Once,
twice,
three times.

Then Mezzo's voice,
sleepy but firm,
drifts over to us from
Cabin Two.
"Cut it out, girls."

"But we're not doing anything!"

Alex waits a moment
before opening the cabin door
and letting it slam shut,
pulling the door to Cabin Two—
attached to ours with fishing line—
along with it.

Bang, bang, bang.

"Girls, I'm not kidding."

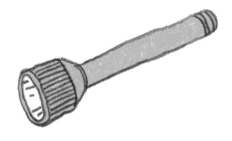

But Mezzo is drowned out
by shrieking,
which means that Rachel and Casey
have risen from their hiding place,
crouched underneath Cabin Two,
and are banging on the floorboards
from below.

Soon the woods
are full of whispers and spinning lights
as Donyelle, Kim, and Becca
crash through the brush
playing ghost.

"Oh for goodness' sake!"

In Cabin Two
the lights go on.

But by the time
Mezzo arrives
at our door

to investigate,
my girls are in bed,
smug smiles
pressed into the pillows.

Taking One for the Team

The next morning
before breakfast
all the Ravens
gather round the firepit
and Kala reminds everyone
that pranks are strictly forbidden.

For the rest of the day
Tex and Mezzo
give me icy looks
and treat me with the cold contempt
reserved for traitors.

But I am warmed
by the attention
showered upon me
by my campers,
who look upon my silence
as a badge of honor,

and by Withers,
who missed all the fun
but looks at me
with new respect.

"Well done, Miss Nova.
I didn't think you had it in you."

Victory

According to my Ravens,
 there is nothing worse
 than being the second-oldest
 unit at camp.

"We're just as mature
 as the Eagles,
 why shouldn't we get
 unlimited flashlight time, too?"

"And a later lights-out time?"

"Plus they get to keep
 their candy in the cabin
 instead of the stupid candy bin!"

I don't have an answer
 that doesn't make me sound
 like their mother.

The Eagles
 have forgotten
 what it's like to be
 second-oldest.

They call the Ravens "kids"
and taunt them
with tales of the sweet life—
Skittles at midnight
and staying up till dawn.

That is when they aren't
ignoring them completely.

Which is why,
at the All-Camp Olympics,
watching Heather
cross the finish line
a full three strides
ahead of the Eagle runner
is sweeter
than all the Skittles
in the world.

Highs / Lows II 🍃

"My high was the Olympics,
 when Heather kicked some Eagle ass."

"Me too!"

"That was my high of the week!"

My high
was the smile
that lit up Heather's face
and continues to shine,
allowing the girls to see her
for the very first time.

Summer Wardrobe

At home
my closet is full
of silk scarves,
vintage slips,
all sorts of beautiful pieces.

Clothes
are sort of my thing.

But you'd never know it
to see me here
in my sun-bleached bikini top
and three-dollar men's undershirts.

It's liberating
to walk around
in the least amount of clothes possible
and not give a second thought
to who might be looking.

A Raven Falls Out of the Nest

Tex passed out
in sports this morning
and is recovering
in the infirmary.

She blamed the heat,
and lack of sleep,
everything
but the diet of
celery and chickpeas
she's been living on
for weeks.

"Don't be late for
our night meeting,"
Kala tells us.

"When Tex gets back
we have some serious
healing to do."

The Recovery Position

That night
we sit in a circle
hand in hand
and Tex starts talking.

"I stopped eating for a bit
in tenth grade.

I'd go out with friends and
feel superior because
they'd be eating whole meals
and all I'd order was water.

Every meal was like a test.
The longer I was able to resist,
the stronger I felt.

But I'd always break down and
eat something in the end."

Tex cries
and we hold tight,
sending her our love,
until she is ready to break
the lightning circle.

She promises to talk to the nurse
and we tell her
how brave she is,
how strong.

When the fire dies
and we call it a night,
there is a peace in Tex's face
I haven't seen in a long time.

I wonder what that feels like.

Tinkle

There's a stowaway
in the bathroom,
second stall
from the right.

Barely a cat.
Mostly fur and bones
and a lot of nerve.

The girls bring her
sausages and
chicken nuggets,
smuggled from the dining hall.

They build her a nest
with stuffing from
Rachel's sleeping bag
and yarn from the activity box.
That yellow stuff no one uses.

They call her Tinkle
and speak in code.

"I'm going to tinkle."

"You should go to tinkle after every meal."

We break their code
and their hearts
by taking Tinkle
to live in the barn.

"Don't worry," says Withers.
"Even the horses
need a good Tinkle
now and again."

TINKLE

Late-Night Riding Lessons

When Withers bursts through the door,
back from a long day in the horse fields,
the girls squeal and rush to greet her.

They trade horsey stories
and I am ignored
like a stay-at-home mom
all but forgotten
by ungrateful children
clamoring for their father's attention
at the end of the workday.

But I don't mind.
I, too, am glad to see Withers.

They pull out their trunks
and mount them like horses.
Withers corrects their posture
and teaches them posting trot.

There,
in the middle of the room,
a makeshift carousel
of grubby girls
atop steamer-trunk steeds
charging toward the future.

Fearless,
for the moment.

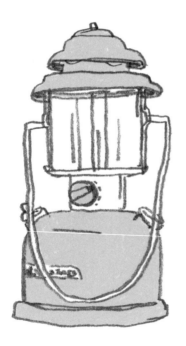

Electricity

I shiver in my sleeping bag
as thunder rolls down the mountain
and crashes through the trees,
barreling straight for me.

Lightning strikes nearby.
It rouses the hairs
on my neck
and arms.

I am more than awake.

The air is alive,
buzzing.
It speaks to me,
filling my head with
electric thoughts
of him.

Early-Morning Secrets

"I need to go to the nurse."

I awake with a start
to find Alex leaning over my bed.
I ask her the standard questions:

"Does it hurt anywhere?"
        "No."
"Are you going to throw up?"
        "No."
"Are you bleeding?"

Alex hesitates,
then shrugs.
Even in the dusky morning light,
my eyes barely open,
I see her cheeks flush.

"Okay, let's go."

Around us the girls shift and sigh
in the loosening embrace of slumber.

        "Wait—"

With a single tug
Alex rips her sheet
from her bed
and crams it into
the nylon sleeve
for her sleeping bag.

She works fast
with her back
between me and the bed,
but I recognize
the rusty odor
and I catch a glimpse
of a dark smear.

"I forgot to put these in the laundry."

I nod
and take the bundle from her.

As we walk in silence
I search furiously
for the right words.
Something from the manual
or, even better,
something from the heart.

At the infirmary
the nurse sees
the bundle under my arm
and understands.

I trade it
for two Midol
and a fresh set of sheets.

She sends Alex to the bathroom
with a pad
and congratulations.

On the way back
I ask if she wants
to call someone.
Her mom, maybe.

"I don't want to tell anyone yet."

"I got my period
during math in sixth grade.
It wasn't what I expected,
more brown than red.
I was the first of my friends
to get it.
I lied
and pretended
I got it a year later
when my friends did."

I've never told anyone
this story before.
It feels good to share,
and I figure one secret
deserves another.

Around us the air rings
with the sounds of a new day,
trunks slamming,
toilets flushing,
counselors yelling,

"Ten minutes, girls!"

Alex pauses at the firepit,
her knuckles as white
as the clean sheets in her arms.

"If anybody asks
we'll tell them you
woke up sweating
and needed new sheets."

Alex nods
and her face relaxes
into an expression
resembling relief.

"But if you need to,
you can talk to me."

The cabin is awake.
We slip in, and immediately
Abby asks, "Where were you?"

"At the infirmary,"
I say.

The girls see
the bare mattress
and nod.

"We were worried," says Abby.

Walking with Kala

In my hour off
Kala and I
go for a river walk.

We leave our shoes
sunning on the rocks
and wade downstream.

Kala glides through life
with the grace
of a heron.

I hop along beside her,
a little brown
sandpiper
scrambling over
rocky terrain.

I love these moments.
Silky green water
cool between my toes,
not a word spoken.

At camp,
a moment of quiet
is a rare moment.

It's nice to share
that moment
with Kala.

Designs by Nova

I splurged
and bought a pack of Sharpies
in candy-colored shades
from the camp store.

I drew all sorts of patterns
across the ribbed cotton
of my men's undershirt collection.

Kim and Becca
are my biggest fans.

"You could sell these, Nova."

"You'd make a killing!"

"I bet they'd let you sell them at the store."

"I'd buy one."

"We wouldn't have to buy them though, right, Nova?"

"We could be your business partners!"

"Yeah, you wouldn't even have to pay us!"

"—just keep us in cool shirts!"

Pretty soon
all the girls are bringing me
T-shirts and bandanas
and asking for custom designs.

Inspired,
I fill out the forms
to request fabric paints and markers
and offer lessons
in Fashion Design
during Arts and Crafts.

In the days that follow,
my chest swells
watching the girls
strut down the winding paths
of Camp Cradle Rock
wearing knockoffs
of my Designs by Nova
Summer 2006 collection.

RACHEL

St. Mary's

I look up from my book
to find Abby
loitering around my bed,
eyes shining.

It takes me a moment
to realize it's tears
that makes them glisten.

In her hand
a postcard trembles.

"I didn't get into St. Mary's."

The sobs that follow
shake her entire body
and sound ugly
in the sweet siesta silence.

St. Mary's
isn't just any private school.
It's the school
her mother,
her aunts,
her sisters
all attended.

The girls approach with caution,
unsettled to see her fall
to Humpty Dumpty pieces.

I tell her I'm sorry
and try to put her back together
with a hug.

"I didn't get into Wellesley."

"I know some girls at St. Mary's.
 You're way too cool for them."

"Yeah. Too cool for school."

"Plus they have the worst uniforms.
 Super-Mega-Fugly!"

"And no boys!"

"So what if they all went?
 You get to be different,
 strike out on your own."

Abby gives us a weak smile,
like sunlight straining
through the clouds.

For the rest of the day
the girls treat her like
a glass angel
balanced at the top
of a Christmas tree.

Fragile
and precious.

Hoedown

Toby Keith
or Keith Urban
or Urban Cowboy

is singing about
heartbreak,
while in the fields
two hundred girls run wild,
drunk on fresh air.

Their fingers are sticky
from sucking on watermelon rinds,
and barbecue sauce
is smeared across their lips
like last night's lipstick.

Winded
from the line dancing,
the three-legged races,
and the belly laughs,

I collapse under a tree
where I have to make space
among all the shoes
the girls kicked off
to dance barefoot in the grass.

Pearls of Hope

Sometimes
I go a whole day
without thinking about him.

But when I do
I remember all the things
I shouldn't.

I chuck away
the bad stuff,
an ocean's worth
of reasons it wouldn't
(and shouldn't)
work,

until all I am left with
are the good moments,
rare, shining, and precious.

I string them along
like pearls
and I wear the necklace
close to my heart,
where it glows
with hope.

The Bear

At night,
I lie awake
listening for the moment
when their breathing
synchronizes.

Someone mutters.
Rachel, maybe.
Above me Donyelle flings a foot
over the edge of her bunk.

Something lands
with a soft thud
at the end of my bed.

A bear,
soft and patchy,
smelling of milk
and skin and fabric softener.

I tuck it into the crook
of Donyelle's arm.
She wraps herself around it,
rubbing her chin against a patch
of fabric worn bare
with years of love.

During the day,
Donyelle hides
any trace of childhood
under thick layers of
lip gloss and sarcasm.

But I know
that somewhere
under the sleeping bag
the bear waits.

The Fall

Kim falls
in slow motion
and lands
with a bounce.

Something crunches
and there's a sickening thud.

Her head, or my heart?

The whistle tastes bitter on my tongue
as I sound the emergency signal

Three!   *Sharp!*   *Blasts!*

that cut through the drone
of camp life.

The girls dismount
and hold their horses at arm's length
while Withers kneels
next to the crumpled body of Kim,
whispering in dove tones.

Lifeguards and riding counselors
spring to action around us,
white backboard
glaring in the sun.

Becca watches from the sidelines,
wailing like a siren,
confusing the nurse,
who asks her where it hurts.

I take Becca's horse
        in one hand
her shoulder
        in the other
and lead them both
toward the barn,
away from her best friend
lying motionless
in the ring.

The White Lady 🍃

That night,
with Kim recovering
in the infirmary,
Becca wants to talk
about The White Lady.

According to legend,
The White Lady
appears to campers
who are sick or in pain.

She never speaks a word,
and no one remembers her face—
only her silhouette,
pale as moonlight,
gliding across the floor.

Alex thinks
she was a nurse
who tended soldiers
during the Civil War.

Casey believes
she was the very first camp nurse,
whose spirit returned
to look after sick campers.

Abby heard
that she was buried on site,
and that one of the gravestones
behind the Arts and Crafts Pavilion
belongs to her.

No one knows for sure.

But they all agree
that she is good,
and that she visits
the infirmary
under the cloak of night,
offering a cool palm
to girls in distress.

In the morning
they awake,
fresh as the dew
on the horse fields.

Leaving the infirmary,
they give their thanks
to the nurse
and offer a silent prayer to
The White Lady.

Cacapon River Queen

One day later
Kim returns to the saddle,
bruised but unbroken,
like a queen to her throne.

Becca and the girls
cluster around her,
ladies-in-waiting
vying for her attention.

I tell her to take it easy
and she gives me a look
of such blue-blooded disdain
that I bow my head.

Withers gives her a leg up
and Kim sits tall in the saddle,
quickly moving to the head
of the trail riders.

Today,
they cross the river
to trail through the fields
on the north side of camp.

I watch
as The Cacapon River Queen leads the way,
leaving us royal subjects
and any lingering fears
behind her.

August

2006

Reconnecting

Mezzo's been having
a rough time.

Kala calls it
the midsummer slump
and says it happens
to the best of us.

After lights-out,
we huddle together
around the dying fire

sharing a can of pop
and a bag of no-name chips
foraged from the kitchen.

"I don't know what's wrong with me.
The girls are sweet, and the staff is great,
but lately all I can think about
is home."

It's funny how our positions have reversed.

Not so many weeks ago
I was the one with the doubts
and Mezzo was the one
telling me to give it some time.

"I feel like we never hang out anymore.
How is that we're in the same unit,
but we never see each other?"

I shrug.

"You and Withers seem really tight.
I never would have guessed it.
She seems so aloof."

"She's not so bad,
once you get to know her."

"Good. Nova?"

"Yes?"

"I'm really glad
you came this summer."

"So am I."

Makeover

At salon night
the girls swarm around Withers,
buzzing about hair, nails, and makeup.

"Can I do your hair, Withers?"

"Do you have any eyeliner?
You'd look so good in eyeliner."

"I'm really good at hair—"

"What about mascara?"

"I won't use a lot of hairspray, I promise!"

"Casey's really good at nails, see?
Look at mine."

"Please, Withers, please?"

Withers snorts
but submits to their
combs and brushes and powders,

and underneath
that stiff upper lip
an English Rose emerges.

"Ta-da!"

"Withers, you're, like, movie star pretty!"

"You should wear makeup more."

"Totally!"

The girls take glamor shots
with disposable cameras
until their reluctant model
pulls back her hair
and wipes the gloss from her lips
to much protesting.

"Come on now,
 if I showed up at the barn like this
 the horses wouldn't recognize me."

And if I hadn't been there
 to witness the transformation,
 neither would I.

Change 🍃

Above me,
two pairs of feet
with watermelon toes
dangle off the bunk.

Across the room,
Rachel writes furiously,
her forehead brushing the page.

Above me,
I hear
the flipping of pages,
the hissing of secrets,
and laughter
muffled into a pillow.

Across the room,
Rachel flinches
but continues to write,
head down.

Last night
and every night before it
I had to force Casey and Rachel
out of Donyelle's bunk
and into their own
long past lights-out.

But tonight,
alone in her own bunk,
Rachel turns her head to the wall
before I even cross the room
to reach the light switch.

Extreme Slip 'n Slide

At announcements
it is officially declared
a Hot Day.

To the girls,
a Hot Day
means one thing.

"When do we get to slip 'n slide?"

The tarp is secured
to a pair of thick-waisted trees
and rolled down
the archery field
like a magic carpet.

We collect tubs of soap,
bubble-gum pink,
and pour them down the tarp
to make it nice and slippery.

Counselors take turns
posted at various parts of the slide
equipped with hoses.

Some girls take it at a run,
flopping onto their bellies
at the last possible second,
careening wildly down the tarp.

Others prefer to sit
on a well-soaped bum,
with a gentle push
to send them on their way.

"Your turn!"
Abby is grinning
and pulling at my sandals,
and before I know it
I'm a link in a human chain.

Gilly goes first,
letting the girls soap her up good.
I grab hold of her ankles
and Tex grabs hold of mine.

The girls give us a shove
and we're off,
speeding along on our stomachs,
sun and water
in our eyes.

We crash into each other,
landing in a soupy mess
of grimy suds
and slimy mud,
scraped and soaked and giddy.

And though I can already feel
the bruises forming on my hips,
I find my footing
in the soggy grass
and head up the hill
to start all over again.

Stains

When I get home,
I will fill the tub
with creamy bath bubbles
and water as hot as I can stand.

I will lounge in it
till I'm pink and wrinkled
and the last of my summer skin
has been scrubbed away.

Then I will slip the straps
of my favorite summer dress
over my clean, shining shoulders
and swirl back into my old life.

But until then
I will soak up the river,
dig my fingers in the sand,
and roll in the grass.

A Bedtime Story

Casey's legs dangle over the bunk
and she leans back
against Donyelle,
who is twisting her hair
into a hundred tiny braids.

"I'm bored,"
Donyelle says.
"Read something."

Casey mumbles
and Donyelle gives a sharp pull
on a freshly twisted braid.

"I can't hear you, Case. Speak up."

"I said I don't want to."

"Don't want to what?"

"Read."

"Don't be a suck.
This is going to take ages.
The least you can do is entertain me."

A hot shade of pink
creeps across Casey's cheeks
and down her neck.

"I don't like to read out loud."

"So?"

"I'm not good at it."

"Who cares?
It's not school.
Just pick something
and read it."

Casey rummages
through a pile of magazines.
Their glossy pages slip
between her trembling fingers.

"No, I wanna hear something good.
Heather, can you throw me a book?
A good one?
Casey's gonna read for us."

Heather looks at Casey
and her shaking hands
and decides on
What My Mother Doesn't Know.

Casey opens the book
and her shoulders relax
as she sees the short lines
swimming in the middle of the page.

She begins to read, slowly at first,
stumbling over the rhythm
and reversing some of the words.

But as she continues
her fingers steady,
and the pinkness fades.

Rachel takes out her earbuds
and Alex looks up from her letter.

One by one
the girls make their way
up to Donyelle's bunk
and find a spot.

They stay like that,
piled like puppies,
despite the heat,
despite the tiny bed,
until it's time
for lights-out.

The Firefighter

In this heat
tempers ignite
like dry kindling.

I spend most of my day putting out fires
caused by heated words.

"God, Heather, don't be such a baby!"

"Leave her alone."

"I wasn't talking to you!"

"We wouldn't have lost if *someone* had actually got in the pool!"

"If you have something to say to me, Becca, just say it!"

" I know you were talking about me at lunch.
Abby heard you."

"So what if we were? It's a free country!
Maybe Abby should mind her own business!"

Mezzo invents a rain dance,
and everyone is so desperate
for a change in temperature
we drop any pretence
of coolness
and run around the fire circle
screaming like five-year-olds:

Drip drop, drip drop
Fiddle dee dee
Rain cloud, rain cloud
Rain on me!

Small Miracles

The sky cracks like an egg
and in seconds we're
soaked through
with warm summer rain.

Kim lifts her face to the sky
and shouts
"Hallelujah!"

After weeks of heat
pressing in at us from all angles
it feels like a miracle
just to walk in the rain.

Rainy Day Dreams

It's been raining
for
three
days.

Riding is canceled.
Sports are canceled.
Aquatics are canceled.

Our girls are excused
from all-camp Bingo
and afternoon showings
of *The Parent Trap*
in the Dance Pavilion.

Instead,
we pull the mattresses to the floor
in one giant plastic island
and share aspirations
and M&M's.

Becca wants to become an actress
and buy a house with an indoor pool.
Kim is going to create a sitcom
for Becca to star in.
Heather would like to be a writer, too—
(books, not TV).
Rachel wants to marry that boy from Casey's magazine
and have beautiful babies.
Alex dreams of being a sportscaster
on a major national network.
Abby sees herself as a doctor in a children's hospital
where she can wear a clown nose,
like Patch Adams.
Casey just wants to get through high school
with a B average and a boyfriend.
Donyelle wants to travel
and wear great shoes.
Withers wants to open a camp in
England and teach
underprivileged girls to ride.

As for me,
I picture an apartment
full of light
and art supplies, and maybe
—someday—
someone kind
making pancakes in the kitchen.

Safe and cozy
in the cocoon of dreams
we've spun around us,
I give myself permission
to put a face to the person
flipping pancakes.

Why not him?
(Why not me?)
People change—
(I've changed).
Nothing
is impossible . . .

especially
on rainy afternoons
made for dreaming.

ME

Looking-Glass Nora

Propped up on my elbows,
pen in hand,
I try to find the words
to describe camp to Kara,

but I don't know where to start.

For the first time
there is a part of me
that Kara doesn't know.

Nova,
the looking-glass Nora,
who knows how
to adjust the girth of a saddle
and counts thirteen-year-olds
and a crusty Brit
among her closest friends.

Nova,
who sings nonsense about
pirates and frogs and Father Abraham,
dances round flagpoles
and traipses around the mountains
in a bikini top and old gym shorts.

If Kara were to press her face
against the looking glass,
would she recognize me?

Her closest friend,
her oldest friend.

Or would I simply remind her
of a girl she used to know?

Morning

I press my face
into the morning,
a damp cloth
that clears my head
and cools my skin.

In the fire circle,
Kala is stretching,
back from her 6:00 a.m. run.

"Good morning,"
she says.
"It's going to be a good day."

The heavy mists
lying over the horse field
dissolve in the early sun
revealing the horses,
noses in wet clover,
glistening with dew.

I watch them feast
before returning to the cabin
to welcome my girls
to a new day.

Mail

"Nova's got a letter from a *boy*!"

My heart stops—
or maybe it starts
—at the familiar return address
partially hidden
by Abby's thumb.

When he told me he'd write,
hope surged through my body
and jump-started the dream
that had sputtered and died.

But day after day
no word came,
and I got used to the idea
that maybe a promise
really is just a bunch of words.

Until now.

Watching the girls examine the envelope
with that familiar, slanted script
hugging the curves of my name

I have to remind myself
to breathe.

Dear Nor,

Sorry I didn't write earlier, but we both know I'm a lazy bastard. How's Camp Crazy Rock? Are you all woodsy now? I still can't believe you chose to spend your whole summer running around after a bunch of rug rats and getting eaten alive by mosquitoes instead of catching double features in the sweet, sweet air-conditioning with yours truly. I'm picturing that episode of *The Simpsons* where the kids are stranded on the island (don't eat the purple berries, they taste like burning! Haha!). Nothing new here, except your old pal has a lady now. Her name is Amy, she came into the store one day during my shift and asked for Monty Python. Can you believe it? A woman after my own heart. She's beautiful and cool and way too good for me. I think you'll like her. In fact, she's the one who reminded me I was being a total asshat and that I should send you a postcard or something before the summer's up. So here you go!

S.C.

What I Know

I know
that people
are talking to me.

I know
the girls
are asking
what's wrong.

But right now
at this moment
I can't
hear
anything

but
her
name.

Heartburn

In the infirmary
I lie awake
throat
eyes
heart
all raw.

In the other room
I hear Kala say something
about exhaustion
and stress.

The nurse comes in
and tells me to rest,
shutting off the lights
and leaving me in semidarkness.

Lying there
I make a silent wish
that The White Lady will come
and press her cool hand
to my burning heart.

a Visitor

"There's someone here to see you."

The nurse shows Mezzo in,
with my dinner plastic-wrapped
on a plastic plate.

"I saved you some apple crisp.
I know it's your favorite."

She refills my water glass
and pulls a chair up
to the bed.

"Are you feeling better?"

I try to speak
but my throat is
all dried out
and rusty.

"We missed you this afternoon.
You should have seen me in Arts and Crafts,
what a mess."

I smile
and start shoveling
apple crisp down my throat
to fill the silences.

"The girls are asking about you.
Are you coming back for campfire tonight?"

I swallow hard
and manage a maybe.

"Well, when you do,
we'll all be there."

The Lightning Circle II

When I return
just after lights-out,
they're sitting in a circle
around the fire
waiting for me.

My very own
lightning circle.

I find a place
close to Withers
and start talking.

I tell them things
I've never told anyone before.
Not even Kara.

How I used to stare at his hands
and imagine them
fifty years from now,
gnarled and spotted
but still full of grace.

How I could barely think
when he sat close to me
because the heat from his skin
fried my brains.

How he took me to the park
the night my grandmother died
and pushed me
on the swing for hours.

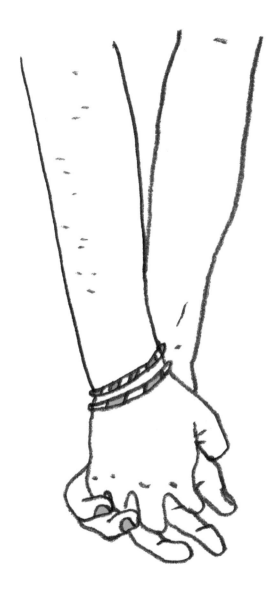

How I told him I loved him
and he said
I was a great girl
but he couldn't imagine us
as anything else
but friends.

I didn't want to be his friend,
but the thought of
not having him in my life
was worse

and so I said I was fine
and took this job
away from home,
away from him.
But I couldn't get away
from myself,

and the secret wish
that he would miss me
and write to me
and tell me he was wrong
and that he had loved me
all along.

When I finish
Kala is holding one hand
and Withers the other,
and the pain
isn't so bad.

Struck

One by one
they tell me about the boys
who broke their hearts,

and I realize that having
your heart broken
isn't all that uncommon,

but having a group of people
to help you through it
is.

Homecoming

I'm careful not to step
on the second stair,
the one that croaks like a frog,
on my way into the cabin.

By now I can make it
through the maze of trunks and shoes
to my corner bunk
without a flashlight.

I slip out of my sandals,
turn back the sleeping bag,
and find eight brightly colored cards
spread like Easter eggs
across the pillow.

Dear Nova,
Sorry you had a bad day.
We missed you tons!
   —Kim
P.S. We wanted to come visit,
   but Kala said no.

Dear Super-Nova (Get it?!),
Get well soon. Kim and I were saying
this was our best summer yet, but not if
you're not here.
   —Yours truly, Becca

Dear Nova,
I never really thanked you for that day
(you know the one I mean), so, thank you.
Get better soon, we miss you.
   —Alex

Dear Nova,
Sorry you had a crappy day.
Boys suck.
Chicks before dicks! Ha ha!
   —Donyelle

Dear Nova,
You are a great counselor and I'm obsessed with your handmade shirts. I'm glad I'm in your cabin. Feel better soon!
—Rachel xoxo

Dear Nova,
I never would have made it past the first week if it wasn't for you. I hope you feel better soon, camp isn't the same without you.

Love, Heather

Dear Nova,
That guy is a jerk. You deserve so much better. I hope you feel better soon.
—Casey

Dear Nova,
You are the best counselor I ever had. I'm sorry for making a big deal about the letter. I didn't know it would be bad. If I did, I would have thrown it into the fire. I hate that I made you cry.

With love from your camp twin, Abby

I read them twice,
then close my eyes
and let their words
lull me to sleep.

Wake-up Call

"Oi, Nova."

Withers is leaning over my bed
fully dressed.

"Get up.
It's time for your lesson."

"My lesson?"

It's then I notice
the riding helmet
and chaps
at the foot of my bed.

"I had to guess your size.
Make sure you wear
boots with a heel.
I'll meet you in the barn."

Withers disappears
out the door
and into the mist
leaving me no choice
but to get dressed
and follow.

Ring Lesson II 🍁

At this hour
the camp feels
like a ghost town,
mist stretching like cobwebs
from tree to tree.

Withers appears,
a solid figure
in the shifting mists,
a palomino at her side.

"This is Flashdance.
Don't worry.
He's not nearly as sprightly
as the name would suggest."

We walk out to a ring
and Withers helps me
tighten the girth
and shorten the stirrups.

Then I'm up
above the mist,
above the ground,
high in the saddle.

Flashdance responds
to the pressure of my knee
in his belly
and the flick of the reins
in my hands,
and together
we walk around the ring.

"Now close your eyes
  and let go of the reins."

"What?"

"He knows you're in control.
  You have to trust him."

"What if I fall?"

"You'll get back on."

I let the reins
slip from my grasp
and I close my eyes.

My heart clip-clops
and I can feel the blood
pulsing in my ears
as my whole body
moves in time with Flashdance,

and for a moment
it's just me
and the horse
and the wind in my face.

"Well done, Nova.
We'd best get back
before the monsters are up."

I dismount,
still buzzing,
and lead Flashdance
back through the mists,
the light of a new day
breaking before us.

God's eye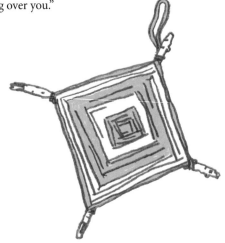

"Time to clean up, girls."

"Nova?"

Heather is beside me
holding the God's eye
I taught her to weave
with scraps of leather
and scavenged twigs.

"This is for you."

"It's beautiful, Heather.
Are you sure you
don't want to keep it?"

"No, I made it for you,
because you're always
watching out for me,
and now it's like someone's
watching over you."

Backstage Battles

Any chink
of spare time
has been taken over
by rehearsals
for the end-of-summer performance.

Kim mounts her trunk,
the one with "Director"
written across the top,
and barks out orders.

"People, people!
We only have three more days!
Three. More. Days."

Casey is not cooperating.
"I told you I don't want to be a man."

"You can't be a woman butler."

"Why not?"

"Because you can't. It's not funny."

"Sexist much? I can be funny and still be a girl."

"It's not sexist, it's British.
There are no girl butlers in British comedy.
That's just the way it is!"

"But we're in America. This is American comedy."

"No, *Murder in the Country* is a British murder mystery!"

"So? You're the writer! Change it!"

"Nova, can you *please* tell Casey
    that it is of utmost importance
    that the butler be a man?"

"Nova, can you *please* tell Kim
    that unless she makes the butler a girl
    I won't be in her stupid play at all?"

"Girls, maybe you should give it a rest
    until tomorrow."

"Fine."

"Fine."

Becca looks up from her script.
"Isn't the theater wonderful?"
    she says.

A Surprise

"You know it's Withers's birthday tomorrow."

I tell Kala
that, no,
I didn't know.

"Good ole Withers.
Doesn't like to make a fuss.
I thought I'd let you know."

I thank Kala
and immediately run off
to tell the girls
the news.

The Reluctant Birthday Girl

At camp,
birthday girls
get an enormous cake
in the flavor of their choice,

big enough
for everyone in the unit
to have seconds.

They also get serenaded
by hundreds of screaming girls
and the honor of wearing
the birthday tiara.

All of these things
(except for the cake)
Withers abhors.

When Withers comes in
we're already in our beds,
giving her the ultimate gift
of silence.

On her bunk
we've laid out
painted horseshoes,
picture frames
made of Popsicle sticks,
and a booklet of coupons
for things like massages
and first dibs
on the showers.

"I told them not to tell anyone,"
Withers says.

Abby throws off her sleeping bag
and protests,

"How can we *not* celebrate your birthday?"

"Well,"
says Withers,

"if you promise not to sing,
I could use one of these massages
right about now."

Hour Off

At eleven-fifteen
I collapse on my cot
and swear that
in my hour off

I will
read a chapter,
write a letter,
complete my
evaluations.

But then the choir
starts to practice.

Their voices rise
and blend,
at first
barely audible
under the bustle
of camp life.

Carried by the breeze,
the song tumbles
down the mountain
like a freshwater stream.

The song flows
under the door
and through the screened windows,
rippling over me
like waves.

An hour later
when I emerge,
there is a buoyancy
to my step
and a lightness
in my smile,
and I return to my girls
refreshed.

Pool Politics III 🍁

"Nova, are you coming in? It's water volleyball!"

The pool is inviting,
a square-cut piece of turquoise
sparkling in a lush green band
of grass.

"I'll play
if everyone plays."

The smile slips
from Abby's face
and she glances at Donyelle,
a few days from home
and yet to get in the water.

Casey and Rachel gave in ages ago,
forfeiting a cool persona
for a cool swim.

"Please, Donyelle?"

Maybe it was the tone in Rachel's voice,
or the hundred-degree heat,
or the battle had finally
grown old,

but something
got to Donyelle.

"Fine. But I want Alex on my team."

Shaving Party

Donyelle is hosting
a shaving party
on the porch.

Rachel, Casey, Abby, and Heather
crowd the steps
at her feet.

Only Donyelle
brought shaving cream,
and so they rub their damp legs
with green apple shampoo,
massaging their ankles
and soaping their knees.

Foamy lather
drips off their legs
in pearly puddles.

Casey lathers her chin
with a beard of bubbles
and Rachel adds
a milky mustache.

Even Donyelle laughs.

The razor looks awkward
in Heather's fist
and she lets Donyelle guide her hand
in the first gentle stroke.

They're admiring their naked, shining legs and
running their hands along each other's shins,
comparing smoothness, when

Becca jumps out
from behind the cabin
and blasts them with the hose.

The girls jump to their feet
and scatter,
rainbow suds and water
flying everywhere.

And when their laughter breaks up
like bubbles on the breeze,
they stretch out on towels
to dry off
in the mellow sunshine.

Performance Night

The whole camp
is sprawled on blankets
in front of the amphitheater.

The riding staff
rush to finish barn duties
and skip dinner
to make it in time.

The sun sets,
casting golden light
over the stage.

By the time the show is over
the stars will be out
to congratulate the performers.

Unit by unit
the girls take to the stage
and show off.

When it's the Ravens' turn
I watch Kim's epic
unfold before my eyes,

a complex whodunit
complete with a butler,
a jilted ex-lover,
and lots of family secrets.

Becca shines as the widow
and Casey has overcome
the injustice of playing the male butler
to deliver a rousing performance.
Heather conquers her stage fright
and is a convincing village vicar.

They know all their lines,
and speak in awful British accents,
peppering their dialogue with
Real British Words,
like minging
and bollocks
and cheeky.

Afterwards,
they take their bows,
big, sloppy smiles
spread like peanut butter
across their faces,

and I swell with pride
for my Ravens
shining brighter
than the late-summer stars.

"Taps"

I've never been big on praying,
but at the end of every campfire,
at the end of every day,
the whole camp stands in a circle,
arms crossed,
and sings,
hand in sticky hand.

After a day
of screaming and laughing
and cheering our throats raw,
"Taps" is whispered,
hovering somewhere between
a lullaby and a hymn.

It's the only song not shouted
but it's as much a part of camp
as bugbites and woodsmoke.

We removed God from the lyrics
(to keep it inclusive)
but I feel a presence
tucking the dusk around us
like a soft gray cloak.

The Last Meal

On the last full day
the sun refuses to get up
and stays wrapped in her
duvet of clouds.

Piece by piece
we take the cabin apart
and pack it away
until all that's left
are the bare bones.

We sort the clothes
on the line,
sweep under the beds,
label things with duct tape.

The girls pass round
their address books
and camp shirts
to be signed.

There should be lots of
talking and laughing and hugging,
but instead

the cabin is thick
with our silence,
heavy as rain clouds,

and when the dinner bell tolls,
we walk the green mile toward
our last meal
like the condemned.

A Kindness of Ravens

In our last nightly meeting,
the girls banging about the cabins
getting ready for candlefloat,
we eat handfuls of cake
straight from the pan
and try to pretend

it isn't the last night
we'll all be together.

We all laugh a little too hard
at Gilly's camper impressions
and insist the wetness in our eyes
is just tears of laughter.

Tex tells us she's gained five pounds
and for the first time
she feels good about it.

Mezzo reads her favorite moments
aloud from her journal
and thanks us all
for a wonderful summer.

Kala sings her latest song,
the one about six girls
who find strength
in each other.

Withers tells her to call it
"The Lightning Circle."

I present everyone
with a custom tank top
and sit back to bask
in the heat of the fire
and the company
of my summer sisters

for
one
last
night.

What I've Gained II

Killer calves
superior s'more-making skills
thirty-six mosquito bites
an appreciation for English chocolate
nine friendship bracelets
a wicked tan
my own clothing line
a binder full of silly songs
    (and some not so silly)
five Popsicle-stick picture frames
    and one God's-eye
a whole new vocabulary of British slang
horseback riding skills
a full address book
perspective.

Candlefloat

The whole camp gathers at dusk,
like reeds upon the riverbank,
to say goodbye.

A single candle
in a block of wood
is floated downstream,
one for each girl.

Our names are read aloud
above the cricket song
and the gurgling river.
Carried by the breeze
they will echo in the mountains
long after we have gone.

It feels a little like
a memorial service,
but I guess that's what it is—

a commemoration
of the time spent
suspended here
in this magical space,
knowing it can never be conjured
quite the same way
again.

Over time
the details will fade,
like our tans
or the Polaroids
we press into scrapbooks,

but the summer lives
in our bodies now,
where it will whisper to us
for the rest of our lives.

Today,
like Alice and Dorothy
and all those other
lost girls before us,
we journey back
through the trees
and into the real world
forever changed.

Acknowledgments

The Lightning Circle is in some ways my most personal book, based loosely on the three summers I spent as a counselor at Camp Rim Rock, an experience that deeply impacted the person I am today. Thank you to Tiffany Gillespie for convincing me to go to CRR that very first summer, and to Jim Matheson, Deborah Matheson Fitzner, Joe Greitzer, and Robin Greitzer for creating such a magical place for girls and women to connect, heal, and grow. I am forever changed by my summer sisters, including Jo-PT, Saralyn, Louisa, Tess, Lisa, France, Leslie, Bev, Rachel, Amy, Suzy, Felicity, and Jolly Jo. Your names echo in my heart still. Thank you to my very first readers, Alison Acheson, Kallie George, Rebecca Jess, Rob Kempson, Anjali Helferty, Haley Rose, and Jennifer MacKinnon—your support and enthusiasm encouraged me to reopen a dusty file after so many years. Thank you to Laura K. Watson for bringing Nora/Nova's sketches to life—the minute I saw your work at TCAF I knew I wanted to work with you. I have endless gratitude for the whole Tundra team, including Tara Walker, Gigi Lau, Bharti Bedi, Kate Doyle, Kelly Glover, Sylvia Chan, Evan Munday, Sam Devotta, Stephanie Ehmann, Catherine Marjoribanks, and Jen McClorey. You make the most beautiful books. To Lynne Missen, I'm so lucky to have you as an editor and even luckier to have you as a friend.

VIKKI VANSICKLE

is the author of a number of acclaimed novels for children including the award-winning *The Winnowing*; *Summer Days, Starry Nights*; and, most recently, *P.S. Tell No One*, as well as picture books, including the bestselling *If I Had a Gryphon*. A former bookseller and marketing director at Penguin Random House Canada, Vikki is a full-time writer, a regular guest on the CTV network talking about books, as well as the education coordinator for The Period Purse, a charity focusing on menstrual equity. She lives in Toronto, Canada, but still dreams about summer camp.

LAURA K. WATSON

is an artist, writer, and zine-maker. She is also the current poet laureate for Tantramar, Canada where she lives with her partner, Patrick, and her cat, Magpie.